# Our Secret

The Sacred Secret is about to get exposed

(Mother and Son's Secret)

## Karena Donger

# Table of Contents

# Content Warning

This book is solely for people who are over the age of legal adulthood due to its sexual content. There are themes with a lot of bad words. All characters are well over the age of eighteen.

*"Oh my god, I'm cuming on your fingers, mommy's cuming. Oh god, what have we done? "*

**- Ellen**

# Free Bonus

**Grab My "At The Beach (Erotic Romance Story)" Ebook For FREE!**

Today you can grab your copy of my Free Erotic Romance story e-book titled – **At The Beach**. Best of all, it won't cost you a thing.

*Download and Subscribe for Free book, giveaways, and new releases by* **Karena Donger.**

Click the image above to **Download the Book**, and also Subscribe for Free books, giveaways, and new releases by me.

Or Follow the link below;

https://mayobook.com/karenadonger

As my subscriber, you will enjoy more free books exclusive to subscribers only, plus **Free Giveaways**. Wait no further, join my growing number of book lovers, and let's connect.

# Our Secret

Tasha, his mother's younger sister, arrived at the house bright and early on Saturday morning.

*"Hi squirt,"* she said. Joel didn't resent the slam; it was a nickname she had given him when he was born.

At the time, she was eight and thought the name was cute. They had always been closer than most nephews and aunts, and with a typical little girl's thought process, she felt it was her duty to help take care of him.

"Hi, Tasha," Ellen and Joel said in unison. "What's up?" his mother (Ellen) added.

Don't you two remember, you promised to help me take some furniture out to the storage shed at Mom and Dad's farm?

Oh, I completely forgot, but it doesn't matter because it's all separated in the back bedroom. She turned to her son. "Can you help Joel?"

"Yeah," he agreed. I've got nothing planned for the day. Sam's out of town and Jeff is sick in bed, so there's no one to hang out with."

As husky as Joel was, it was still a lot of work to load the bed, chest, and boxes from their house into the pickup. They began loading the pickup truck with those furniture and boxes.

Finally, after two hours, they were ready to go. Joel covered the load because it looked like it was going to rain, and even had to move a couple of the boxes inside the truck, setting them on the seat behind Tasha.

"You're going to have to sit on Joel's lap," Tasha said to Ellen. As she was to drive the truck "There won't be enough room to sit because of these boxes, and other loads."

*"That will be alright, won't it Joel?"* his mother said.

"Well, as long as you don't weigh a ton and take up

the whole side of the truck," he said, laughing.

"I'll have you know I weigh one hundred pounds, young man, and I'm only five foot tall, not six foot three." She was grinning when she said it, but there was a little bit of pride in her voice.

At thirty-nine, his mother had the body and looks of a high school senior. Although few high school girls had 36C boobs that were full, firm, and had such prominent nipples, plus a number ten ass.

Calling his attention to her body was not the best thing she could have done.

He settled himself in the seat and she hopped in and, placing her feet between his, she lowered herself to his lap.

She was wearing a thin summer dress, and he had seen only a bikini panty line and a bra under it. He immediately felt the heat from her body flow into his crotch area.

He turned his mind to the road ahead.

Tasha pulled away, and moments later they were on the country road to the farm, twenty miles away.

The road was under construction for more than five miles, and the truck bounced with a steady rhythm as it rolled along the ridges left by the road grader.

Tasha and Ellen kept up a constant chat about women things, leaving Joel with his own thoughts.

In time, he became aware of the rhythmic bouncing and the heat coming from his mother's ass as it pressed against his crotch, which made him feel hot.

Suddenly, to his horror, his cock began responding to the movement. He felt the first stirrings of a hard-on. He tried to think of other things, but the more he tried thinking of other things, the more he thought of his cock.

Gradually, his dick became firmer and began to rise, until it was contained by the ass pressing down on it. This pressure only succeeded in causing it to become more rigid until it was like a bar of steel. He could feel the crack between his mother's legs, and finally, her pussy, as the rigid shaft forced itself against the spread lips of her ass.

There was no doubt she could feel the hard bar against her panty-covered ass, but she made no motion or comment that indicated she was aware of his predicament.

Ellen first ignored the hard rod pushing against her ass. Then, without thinking, she adjusted herself slightly and the pressure switched directly to her pussy.

In the beginning, she was irritated that her own son would get an erection from her sitting on his lap. But the more she thought about it, the funnier it became.

What a waste of a good hard-on she thought; getting rigid for your mother. Ellen almost laughed out loud. The bouncing of the seat, caused the hard member to slip back and forth along her ass.

Then a sudden bump drove his cock head against her,

forcing her panties and thin dress between her thigh for just a split second.

A minute later, thinking about the incident, Ellen realized that technically, for that split second, her son's cock had been touching her pussy.

True, it had just been the very tip and it had been covered by panties and a dress, but was that any different than being covered by a condom?

The thought was so erotic, that her pussy flooded with moisture. She had certainly never considered her son a sexual being or partner. In fact, her husband had a stroke three months ago, and the doctor told her not to have sex with her husband for six months going forward. She wasn't sexually frustrated. Her husband's fingers and her vibrator had provided all the sex she required.

The bouncing cock rubbing against her pussy slowly demanded her full attention. She couldn't help but squeeze her ass cheeks together to try to close her vagina opening, but it had the opposite effect.

It reminded her that a twenty-year-old cock was thrusting itself against the lips of her wet pussy.

Ellen felt what she thought was an answering thrust from Joel's penis to her movement.

*"Why is that little brat coming on to me by flexing his cock against me,"* she wondered.

But instead of getting angry, she actually responded again by pushing against his rising rod. Minutes later, they whipped into the drive at the farm, and Ellen breathed a sigh of relief.

She had been dangerously close to starting something that could have ruined both their lives.

The road got a little rougher and the motion of the truck added a side-to-side sway to the jogging motion. Joel would have sworn the heat coming from her thighs and ass increased more and more. It couldn't have been more like fucking if they had been in a bed. Just when he was about to blow his load all over, they turned into the farm drive and the truck rolled to a stop.

"There," said Tasha, "that wasn't so bad a trip, was it?"

*"I thought it was a perfect road trip,"* his mother said. She turned on his lap, grinding her ass against his hard cock, and slowly slid out of the truck to the ground, her dress sliding up until her panties were just peeking from underneath.

"I don't think Joel minded a bit. Did you honey?" *She turned to him and winked.*

He couldn't believe what she had said.

*"Ah, no, I agree with you, it was just perfect. The time just flew by,"* he said.

"Great," Tasha said, "Why don't we go in and see where Dad wants this stuff put.

"Joel," his mom said, *"Why don't you stay out here and, ah, maybe untie the covering, you know, get things settled down."* Her eyes flicked to his crotch and returned to his face.

He blushed when he realized his hard-on was standing out, tent-like, from the front of his shorts.

*"Okay, I'll... I'll get things ready to carry in,"* he stammered.

She grinned and walked around the truck to join Tasha on her way to the house.

Within twenty minutes, the load was in the house, and they were ready to start going back home. But as usual when they visited grandma, she insisted they take some home-canned fruit home with them, so they ended up with three large cardboard boxes.

Just as they were loading them, it began to rain. Grandpa suggested we put the boxes in the truck to keep the cardboard from getting wet and falling apart, so once again there were boxes taking up the middle of the truck seat and Ellen had to ride on Joel's lap again. What a coincidence, as Tasha would have to drive.

They started

Within a short distance, Joel's cock achieved its original proportions and began rubbing her pussy. There was little doubt that he knew it was exciting for her.

If her panties hadn't slipped into her crack, and began rubbing her clit each time the truck bounced his cock against her, she would have been able to keep herself under control.

Actually, Ellen accidentally made the first thrust. Although later, she was to wonder if it had all been an accident. Her leg was falling asleep because of the odd angle she was holding it, and she raised her foot slightly to move it. The resulting loss of support for her ass allowed it to rest heavier on her son's cock.

When he pushed back in response, she was unable to keep her wet pussy from answering the hard rod tapping at its portal.

The trip home was slower due to the rain, but just as

rough, and within the first mile, his hard-on was back in full force. His mom adjusted her ass so his rigid cock fit exactly between her legs and his cock was thrust tightly against her pussy. After a few rough jolts, he felt what appeared to be a soft push downward against his penis from his mom's ass.

It was hard to tell. He waited for a moment, then was sure he felt another push. For fear of being pushed, he was imagining things, doing a lot of wishful thinking. Then it happened again, and there was little doubt his mom was pushing her pussy against his hard-on. In answer, he flexed his cock.

He knew the movement would be so minor she would barely feel it, but if she had pushed, it would be enough, if she hadn't it wasn't so strong that it would feel like he was trying to fuck her if he had guessed wrong.

Immediately he felt an answering push. He answered with a strong thrust toward her pussy. Her response was immediate, and within seconds they were dry fucking. The boxes stacked between his aunt, him and his mother prevented her from seeing anything but their heads and shoulders. They were keeping the thrust below their waists. Joel first placed his hands on his mom's hips, then finally he reached around her and laid them on her thighs. Ellen inhaled sharply, but she continued to thrust her ass against his cock and flex her ass muscles, which was squeezing Joel's cock like a hand.

Joel began to slowly pull her skirt up her legs. He hoped to get his fingers under her panties for a quick feel. Just when Joel was about to blow his white cum in his shorts, they arrived back at their drive.

Ellen again twisted on his cock and slipped to the ground exposing her crotch-wet panties to him. He followed her out, and she reached for one of the boxes on the seat and handed it to Joel.

Here, honey, you can take this to the kitchen for me. Her smile told him she was again giving him a way to keep his hard-on out of sight.

"Thanks for all your help, you guys, I'll see you both get a reward for the effort," she said laughing.

*"Hey, we enjoyed it. It was fun," Ellen said."*

"I think Joel especially enjoyed the drive." Said Tasha.

Yeah, Aunt Tasha, I really enjoyed going out to the farm. It's fun to ride in a truck for a change instead of a car, it bounces around like a ride at Disney Land. "

"If they had rides like that at Disney Land," Ellen said, *"I'd have been there a long time ago."*

"Ah, you know what I mean, like a once in a lifetime thrill," he said.

"That I agree with," she said. Ellen was sure that it was in fact a once-in-a-lifetime thrill. It certainly couldn't go any further.

Joel carried the box inside and set it on the counter, then went into the room and grabbed the remote. He flicked the remote twice, and MTV started blasting from the screen. He chose a straight chair because he knew his mother would say something if he sat on the sofa in dirty shorts. Ellen followed him into the room. She stopped next to him.

"You didn't mind my sitting on your lap, did you?"

*"No, mom. Like I told Aunt Tasha, the trip was a once-in-a-lifetime thrill."*

"And my weight didn't bother you?"

*"Mom, you don't weigh anything. I could hold you all afternoon and it wouldn't bother me. "*

"Oh really? Maybe I'll take you up on that and sit on your lap now. "

Joel quickly looked up at her.

*"I... I wouldn't mind that at all."*

Ellen stared at him for a minute. My god, she thought, what am I doing? This is my son. If I sit on his lap, things are going to get out of hand. But her inner self convinced her that she was old enough to keep the situation from going past the point of mother and son joking around. Her eyes locked on his for a moment, then she stepped in front of him, and sat down on his lap. But this time her legs were outside Joel's and she was more open and exposed.

Joel couldn't believe that his mother had just spread herself and sat on his lap. It was an instant hard-on.

His cock rose quickly to lodge itself against her pussy, covered only by her thin dress and panties.

A moment later, she pushed down against his rigid boner, as she had been doing in the truck.

Joel thrust back. He makes little pretence of doing anything but pushing his cock against her pussy. She returned his thrust with one of her own. The thrusting continued, and there was no sham between them; they were dry fucking.

Joel reached his arms around Ellen (his mom) and laid his hands on her thighs. She looked down at them but said nothing. She was panting hard as she worked her ass against his hard member.

Joel began clutching bunches of her skirt in his fingers and, slowly, her skirt crept up her legs. Ellen watched her tanned legs become more exposed, but it felt like it was happening to someone else. Her mind was concentrating on the hard cock pressing against her inflamed pussy lips.

Finally, her panties came into view, and the dress continued up her body until Joel had bunched it at her waist. He lowered his hands back to her thighs and laid them with fingers pointing in on her legs just below her pussy.

Ellen stared but said nothing. Slowly his hands moved up, and she gasped as they touched her panty-clad mound.

Joel rubbed his mother's pussy and smeared the wet juice he found there around until her whole crotch was soaked in her flowing liquid. As her lips spread, he let his fingers move between them. He then traced an outline from the bottom of the puffy lips to her clit, which was clearly visible against her wet panties.

He flicked his finger against the nubbin, and Ellen groaned.

Joel lifted his hands and, pulling the waistband of her pants out with one hand, he slipped his other hand against her trembling belly and slid it down to her pussy.

Stopping there, he turned his palm upward and, with his other hand, thumbed her panties down over her hips.

Ellen's eyebrows were raised slightly as the panties slipped under her ass and crept to her knees. Joel didn't bother to remove them entirely. He liked to see the panties there to remind him that she was naked below the waist.

He pulled his hands back up her legs, and Ellen watched in awe as her son buried his fingers in between the puffy lips of her pussy, spreading them and slowly inserting two of his fingers into her channel.

Ellen's orgasm roared through her like a train through a tunnel, the sheer force scattering debris on both sides. She roared like an animal, huffed and puffed, and hunched her back on his fingers.

*"Oh my god, I'm cuming on your fingers, mommy's cuming. Oh god, what have we done? "*

Joel didn't wait for an answer. He lifted her up, forcing her to her feet while she was still out of control, and tore the buttons from his shorts, releasing his massive cock.

With much effort, he managed to pull the throbbing monster from his underwear, and suddenly there under Ellen was his eight-inch pillar of flesh, red-headed and throbbing.

The orgasm was so intense that Ellen didn't even know what Joel was doing. She was still foaming at the mouth and could barely stand in the position he had her in. Joel lowered her ass slowly. As she sat down, he positioned his cock directly below her dripping pussy. Ellen thought it was his fingers spreading the still burning lips of her hot cunt. But they kept spreading and spreading, and suddenly reality ate through her fogged brain.

She screamed. *Joel, No. No, you can't fuck me. "*

Joel released his support of her ass. With nothing holding her up and with her legs too weak to support her, she slipped down the massive shaft, taking the nine-inch cock into her saturated depths.

*Oh, Ohh my god.* Joel, *oh my God, you're so big.*

*Ohh, you shouldn't be putting your cock in me. I'm your mother.*

*"Ellen's fall was stopped by Joel's legs. She was firmly impaled by the hard cock. "Unhh," she grunted."*

Joel immediately lifted her a little and dropped her again on his shaft. burying it in her womb. Then again and again. It was a very hard fuck by Joel. He fucked the hell out of his mom's wet pussy.

Moments later, Ellen was assisting him by raising and lowering herself on the red meaty pole. A couple of strokes later, Ellen's fingers strayed to her clit, and she began rubbing the stiffened little knob.

*"God, Joel, you're a stud, a fucking horse."*

*Mom, I'm going to cum. I'm going to shoot. I'm going to shoot. "*

Ellen threw her head back against Joel's shoulder.

*"Me too, baby.* Your cock is making me cum again. She said.

*"Cum in my pussy, honey. Cum in mommy's cunt. "*

*"Ohhh, Mommmmm."* Joel's cock spewed hot white threads of cumin into her.

Shoot your juice in, honey, shoot your juice in, mommy. Bury it in me. *"Uhhhhh."*

*"Oh my god, you're fucking,"* Tasha screamed out.

*"Joel, you're really fucking your mother?"*

Ellen slumped back against Joel as her orgasm drifted off its peak.

She turned her head toward the voice coming from the kitchen door. "Not really, Sis," she said.

"You're wrong. We're really fucking each other, and if you think I'm going to let him take that massive cock out of me just because you've caught us, you're wrong. You can either watch and finger fuck yourself, or turn your head. " – **Ellen responded**.

Ellen turned as far around as Joel's cock would let her and planted a kiss full on her son's lips, her tongue slipping inside.

*"Honey, your cock still feels hard. Why don't you fuck mommy again? We'll sort this all out later after we fuck. Unless you don't want to do it again."*

For an answer, Joel lifted his mother's ass up about five inches, then dropped her.

Again, she was impaled on the massive rigid cock."

"Oh, honey. "Mommy loves the way you answer," she cooed.




…Continue to Series 4




What do you think would happen after Tasha caught Joel fucking his mom so hard, and what would Ellen do to keep this sacred secret from getting revealed by her sister?


*Check out the continuation of this story in the fourth book in the series Our Secret 2 (Mother and Son's Secret 4).*

# Thank You!

# Free Bonus

**Grab My "At The Beach (Erotic Romance Story)" Ebook For FREE!**

Today you can grab your copy of my Free Erotic Romance story e-book titled – **At The Beach**. Best of all, it won't cost you a thing.

*Download and Subscribe for Free book, giveaways, and new releases by* **Karena Donger.**

Click the image above to **Download the Book**, and also Subscribe for Free books, giveaways, and new releases by me.

Or Follow the link below;

https://mayobook.com/karenadonger

As my subscriber, you will enjoy more free books exclusive to subscribers only, plus **Free Giveaways**. Wait no further, join my growing number of book lovers, and let's connect.

# About The Author

I'm a romance writer and I've been writing for 10+ years. I write dark and romantic erotica. I have a penchant for romance. I also have a fondness for writing stories that inspire, and a love for the genre of romantic fiction. I write dark and erotic romance because I love the power of darkness and the eroticism that comes with it. I love the passion and the desire. I love the way a man will stop at nothing to get what he wants.

I also write fantasy and contemporary romance because I love the magic and adventure of it, coupled with the modern world and the characters in it. I love the modern family and modern relationships.

I have always loved reading romance novels, and now I am writing them too. I hope to share my love of romance with readers through my writing.

Visit https://mayobook.com/karenadonger to download my Free Erotic story **"At The Beach"** Today!

# Other Books

1. The Road Trip (Mother and Son's Secret Book 1)

2. The Road Trip 2 (Mother and Son's Secret Book 2)

3. Our Secret (Mother and Son's Secret Book 3)

4. Our Secret 2 (Mother and Son's Secret Book 4)

5. The Road Trip Secret, Complete Series Box Set (Mother and Son's Secret)

www.ingramcontent.com/pod-product-compliance
Lightning Source LLC
Chambersburg PA
CBHW060602100726
47907CB00005B/1485